Put Beginning Readers on the Right Track with
ALL ABOARD READING™

The All Aboard Reading series is especially for beginning readers. Written by noted authors and illustrated in full color, these are books that children really and truly *want* to read—books to excite their imagination, tickle their funny bone, expand their interests, and support their feelings. With four different reading levels, All Aboard Reading lets you choose which books are most appropriate for your children and their growing abilities.

Picture Readers—for Ages 3 to 6
Picture Readers have super-simple texts with many nouns appearing as rebus pictures. At the end of each book are 24 flash cards—on one side is the rebus picture; on the other side is the written-out word.

Level 1—for Preschool through First Grade Children
Level 1 books have very few lines per page, very large type, easy words, lots of repetition, and pictures with visual "cues" to help children figure out the words on the page.

Level 2—for First Grade to Third Grade Children
Level 2 books are printed in slightly smaller type than Level 1 books. The stories are more complex, but there is still lots of repetition in the text and many pictures. The sentences are quite simple and are broken up into short lines to make reading easier.

Level 3—for Second Grade through Third Grade Children
Level 3 books have considerably longer texts, use harder words and more complicated sentences.

All Aboard for happy reading!

To Megan at four

Library of Congress Cataloging-in-Publication Data

Dubowski, Cathy East.
     Snug Bug's play day / by Cathy East Dubowski ; Mark Dubowski, [illustrator].
        p.   cm.—(All aboard reading. Level 1)
     "Preschool-Grade 1."
     Summary: Snug Bug discovers that he can have more fun at the playground if he shares.
     [1. Insects—Fiction. 2. Sharing—Fiction. 3. Play—Fiction. 4. Stories in rhyme.]
I. Dubowski, Mark, ill. II. Title. III. Series.
PZ8.3.D8525Sp   1997
[E]—dc21   97-8290
                                                                                    CIP
                                                                                     AC

ISBN 0-448-41642-5 (GB)   A B C D E F G H I J

ISBN 0-448-41623-9 (pbk.) A B C D E F G H I J

ALL
ABOARD
READING™

Level 1
Preschool-Grade 1

Snug Bug's Play Day

By Cathy East Dubowski
and Mark Dubowski

Grosset & Dunlap • New York

Snug Bug is sleeping—
snug as a bug in a rug.
Mama Bug gives
his covers a tug.

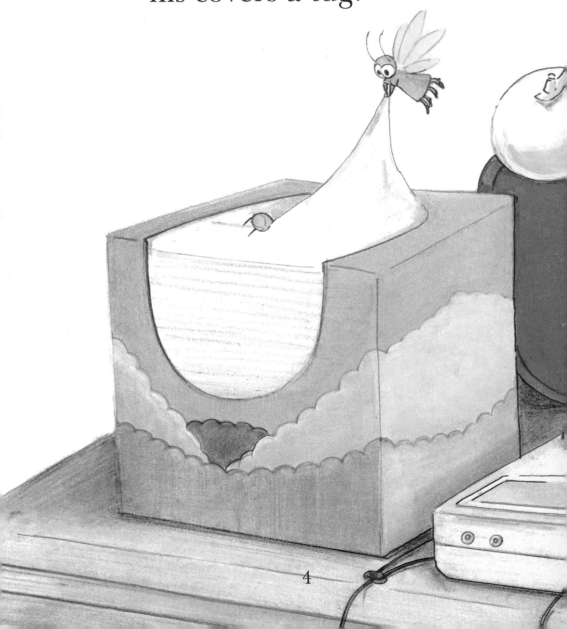

Snug Bug hides.

Mama tickles his toe.

She wakes him up
with the radio.

Snug Bug hurries
to get dressed.

Here is the shirt
that he likes best.

He puts his shoes
on all four feet.

Then Mama says,
"It's time to eat!"

Snug Bug sits
while Mama makes
toast and jam
and Yummy Flakes.

Now it's time
to go and play.
Snug Bug leads the way.
Hooray!

In the sand,
Snug Bug makes
a treat for Mama—
sandy cakes.

This little ring
can swing so high.
Snug Bug swings
up to the sky!

A little bug says,
"It's my turn now!"
But Snug Bug
stays on anyhow.

"Take turns," says Mama.
Snug Bug frowns.
He does not want to,
but he gets down.

He wants to climb
the jungle gym.
But there is
no room for him.

So Snug Bug says,
"I will try the slide."
But Little Bug is next
in line to ride!

He cuts off Little Bug
and flies to the top.
Little Bug shouts,
"No fair! Stop!"

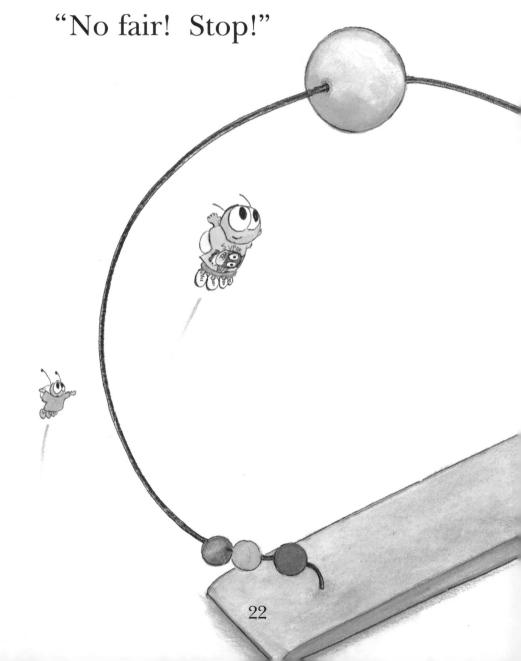

Snug Bug giggles!
"Look at me!
Here I go!
Whee!"

Look! A seesaw!
But Snug Bug frowns.
The seesaw won't
go up and down!

It needs a bug
at the other end.
Snug Bug needs
a little buggy friend.

What do you think
Snug Bug will do?
He asks Little Bug
to seesaw, too.

Snug Bug says,
"I will be nice."
Little Bug makes him
promise twice.

Now the seesaw
works just right.
It was very silly
to have a fight.

"Time to eat!"
the mamas say.
"Let's have our lunch
right here today."

One has peanut butter.
One has jelly.
They make a wish
and then they...

...SQUISH!

Peanut butter and jelly.
A yummy way
for two new friends
to share their day.